WALT DISNEY'S
Brer Rabbit Plays Some Tricks

GROLIER
BOOK CLUB EDITION

Brer Wolf and Brer Fox and Brer Bear all loved rabbit stew.

So they were always trying to catch Brer Rabbit.

But Brer Rabbit was too smart for them.
He always had a trick up his sleeve.

Now one day
Brer Rabbit decided
to build himself
a house.

His first house was made
of straw.

It was a nice house—
until Brer Fox tore it down.

His second house was
made of bark.

It was a nice house
too—until Brer Wolf
blew on it.

His third house was made of reeds.

It was just as fine as could be—
until Brer Bear sat on it.

Finally Brer Rabbit
realized that he needed
a proper house
made of wood...

with a stone chimney...

and doors and windows
with locks.

At last Brer Rabbit knew peace and quiet.
He could live like other folks.
And he did—for a while.

Then one day Brer Rabbit went off
and left his front door wide open.
Along came Brer Fox.

When Brer Fox
saw that open door,
he began to think
about rabbit stew
for supper.

He went inside and closed the door.
Then he hid behind a chair and waited
for Brer Rabbit to come home.

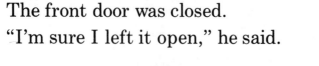

By and by Brer Rabbit returned.
Right away he knew something was wrong.
The front door was closed.
"I'm sure I left it open," he said.

Brer Rabbit
peeked in
the window.
But he
could not
see anything.

He looked down the chimney too.
All he saw was a lot of soot.

He even listened
at the wall, but he
did not hear a sound.
Still, he did not
go into the house.

Instead, Brer Rabbit climbed a tree
and hollered out, "HEY-HO, HOUSE!"

When Brer Fox heard this,
his eyes grew big and wide.

The house did not answer.
So Brer Rabbit hollered again,
"HEY-HO, HOUSE! WHY AREN'T YOU TALKING?"

"HEY-HO YOURSELF!"
called Brer Fox.
He tried to sound
like a house.

"THAT'S NOT HOW A HOUSE TALKS, BRER FOX!"
yelled Brer Rabbit.

Brer Fox thought he was losing his mind.
Maybe that house really could talk!
He did not wait around to find out.
Off went Brer Fox—lickety-split!

So Brer Rabbit stayed out of the stewpot THAT night.

But the next day he almost jumped in.

Brer Wolf had thought of a trick.

First he dug a hole next to a big rock.

Next he lay down in the hole and pulled
the big heavy rock over him.

Then he listened for Brer Rabbit.

By and by Brer Rabbit came
dancing down the road.

"HELP! HELP!"
called Brer Wolf.

Brer Rabbit heard
him and stopped.

"What can I do for you, Brer Wolf?" asked Brer Rabbit.

"I'm trapped under this rock," said Brer Wolf. "Get me out if you can."

Brer Rabbit was always glad to help
a neighbor.

He pushed and shoved and shoved and pushed—
until he moved that rock off poor Brer Wolf.

Brer Wolf jumped up and grabbed Brer Rabbit.
But Brer Rabbit was not really scared.
He knew a few tricks of his own.

"You can't grab the one who saved your life,"
said Brer Rabbit. "It's a law."

"I never heard of that law," said Brer Wolf.

"Then ask Brer Bear," said Brer Rabbit.
"If I'm right, you have to let me go.
If I'm wrong, you can eat me."

"Well...all right," said Brer Wolf.

Brer Bear listened to both sides.

"Come on, Brer Bear," said Brer Wolf.
"Tell him you never heard of that law."

"Brer Bear is not dumb," said Brer Rabbit.
"He can't decide until he sees the hole."

Brer Bear looked at the hole.

"Come on, Brer Bear," said Brer Wolf.
"We all know there is no such law."

"Brer Bear is not stupid," said Brer Rabbit.
"He can't decide until he sees how you were
trapped under the rock."

Brer Wolf put down Brer Rabbit and lay down in the hole and pulled the rock over him.

"Hurry up, Brer Bear," he said. "This rock is heavy."

Brer Bear looked at Brer Wolf.
"I think I know the answer now," he said.

"You were wrong, Brer Rabbit," he said.
"You had no business helping Brer Wolf.
You should have left him under the rock."

"I have learned my lesson," Brer Rabbit
said as he danced on down the road.
"I will never help Brer Wolf again."

Brer Bear thought he had been a mighty fine judge that day.

But his friends set him straight.

"Brer Rabbit tricked you," said Brer Fox. "You helped him get away."

That made Brer Bear mad.

So the next day he caught Brer Rabbit.

"You know what I do to folks who fool me?" said Brer Bear. "I knock them dead."

When he heard this, Brer Rabbit started to laugh.

"Why are you laughing?" asked Brer Bear.
"I just said I was going to knock you dead."

"I know, I know," said Brer Rabbit.
"But I can't help thinking
about my laughing place."

"How come you have a laughing place?" said
Brer Bear. "I don't have a laughing place."

"Some folks are rich, some folks are poor,"
said Brer Rabbit.

"Hmmm," said
Brer Bear.
"Show me
this place."

So off they went until they came to
a place where the bushes grew thick.
Brer Rabbit pointed to a tunnel
in the bushes.

"That's it?" cried Brer Bear. "How
come I don't feel like laughing?"

"All you have to do is run straight through that tunnel," said Brer Rabbit. "Then the laughing begins."

"If you say so," said Brer Bear.

Brer Bear took off.

He ran through the tunnel just as
fast as he could go.

He ran so fast, he ran right into
a hornets' nest.

Were those hornets mad!!
They started to sting Brer Bear.
"OW...YOW...OUCH...YIKES!" he yelled.

Brer Bear came running out of the bushes.
The hornets chased him around and around.
Brer Rabbit laughed so much, his sides
began to hurt.

At last Brer Bear escaped from
the hornets.

"Say, I didn't see anything funny
in there," he said. "I thought this was
a laughing place."

"HO HO HO HA HA HA!" went Brer Rabbit.

"I didn't say this was YOUR laughing place," said Brer Rabbit.

"I said it was MY laughing place—and I've been laughing ever since I got here."

And before Brer Bear knew that he had
been tricked again, Brer Rabbit was gone!